THIS Picture Knight BOOK
BELONGS TO

CALUM Lorimer

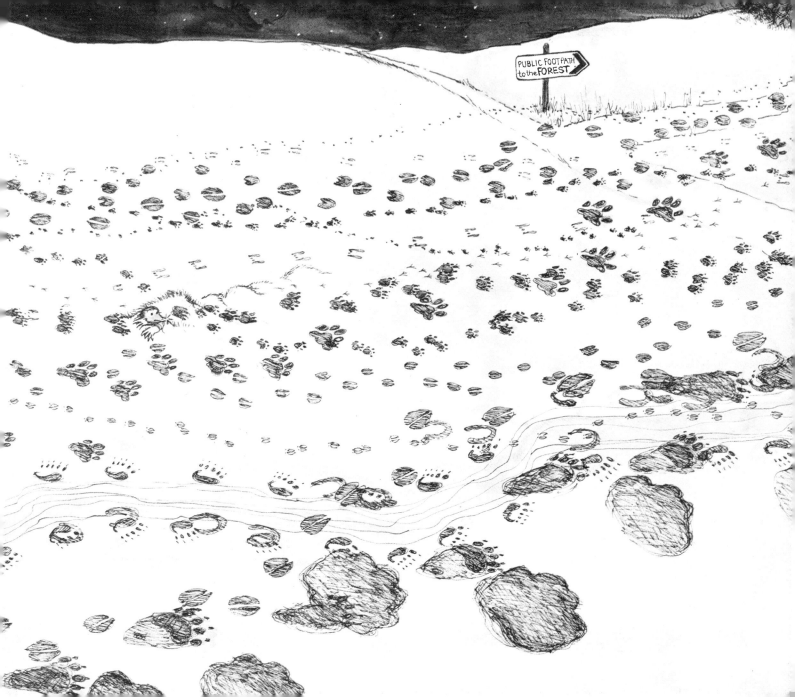

PUBLIC FOOTPATH to the FOREST

For Alexander the Small
and Denny the Slim

ANIMAL DAY

by Neil Hollander
Illustrated by Susanna Gretz

Picture
Knight

HODDER AND STOUGHTON

British Library Cataloguing in Publication Data

Hollander, Neil
  Animal day.
  I. Title   II. Gretz, Susanna, *1937*–
823′.914[J]

  ISBN 0-340-48694-5

Text copyright © Neil Hollander 1987
Illustrations copyright © Susanna Gretz 1987

First published 1987 by Hodder and Stoughton Children's Books
This edition first published 1988 by Picture Knight
Second impression 1989

Published by Hodder and Stoughton Paperbacks,
a division of Hodder and Stoughton Ltd,
Mill Road, Dunton Green, Sevenoaks, Kent TN13 2YA
Editorial office: 47 Bedford Square, London WC1B 3DP

Printed in Great Britain by Springbourne Press, Basildon, Essex

It was the biggest gathering of animals since Noah loaded his ark.
Every kind of bird and beast was there: wild animals,
work animals, circus animals, tame animals.
They all came to the forest in the middle of the night
to decide what to do.

The lion spoke first.
"People have ruled us long enough,"
he said. "Now, it's our turn!"

"Make them work,"
said the bull.

"Let them pull the carts,"
laughed the horses.

"We'll take them for
walks," barked a dog.

"And make them
jump through hoops!"
growled the tiger.

"Vote,"
said the goats.
"Let's vote on it."

The animals all raised their wings or flippers or paws or hooves in agreement.
"Long live the animal kingdom," the elephant trumpeted.

While the people slept, the animals took over.
Moles, mice and cats of every kind crept quietly
through the houses collecting all the keys.
They took the keys to everything: the houses,
the factories, the offices and shops – even
the keys to barns and bicycles.

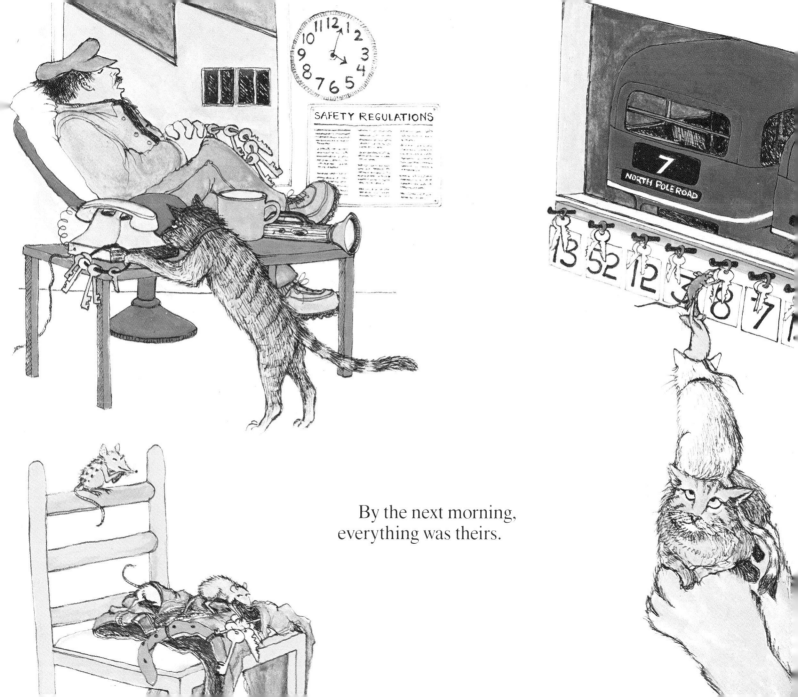

By the next morning,
everything was theirs.

When the people woke up, the world was very different.

"From now on, you'll live here," said the stallion as he led the farmer to the stable.

"You'll sleep in my house," the dog told his former owner.

ROVER

PUSSYKINS

"And eat out of my bowl," added the cat.

But when the animals moved in,
they discovered they had to make a few changes.

The beds were too short for giraffes, the chairs too high for
hedgehogs and turtles, the doors too narrow for buffaloes, and the
bathtubs far too small for crocodiles.

A pack of beavers set to work, making things bigger
and smaller, shorter and taller, wider and narrower.
Finally everything fitted, and the animals felt at home.

Every animal found a job to do:
Zebras directed traffic.
Birds delivered mail.
Foxes drove taxis.
Kangaroos swept streets.
Giraffes washed windows.

Elephants became firemen.
Skunks collected garbage.
Penguins sold ice cream.
And, of course, the lion was king.
    "Today is Animal Day,"
trumpeted the elephants.

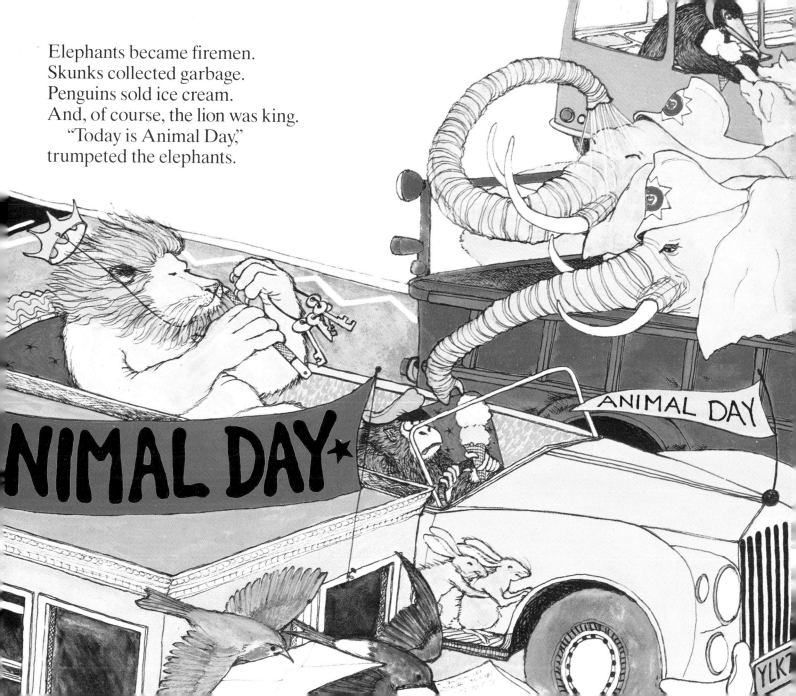

On the farms, people now did the work.
Early in the morning a farmer
climbed to the top of the barn and cried,
"Man-o-doodle-do!" again and again until
everyone woke up. Then all day people
towed the carts, hauled the hay, and
pulled the ploughs.

The biggest and strongest men
wore saddles on their shoulders. Shouting
"Giddy-up and go," monkeys rode them
everywhere.

"Go and pick me a bushel
of grass," said Boss Bull
to his herd of farmers.
"Just the juicy, tender tops,
mind you.
No roots, and no dirt!
And don't chop them up either.
You know how much I like to
chew them myself."

At the zoo, people now lived in the cages. In the noisiest one were the *Blaboons* – lawyers, politicians, and teachers – who were always chattering and arguing with each other. Nearby, their cousins, the *Doodleloons* – bankers, businessmen, and bureaucrats – scribbled and scrambled huge stacks of paper.

Most popular of all was the Children's Corner of the zoo, where boys and girls played on swings and slides and begged for popcorn and peanuts.

Crowds of animals came to look at the different kinds of people.

The animals discovered that people made good pets, and nearly every family had one or two.

"Shake hands," said Police Chief Panda Bear to his pet person. "That's it. Good boy. Now, roll over, and I'll give you a chocolate bone."

"I'm going shopping," Mrs Hippo told her pet girl.
"You watch the house while I'm gone. Don't make a mess,
or too much noise. And remember – stay off the furniture!
If you behave, I'll take you for a walk when I come back."

PEOPLE SHOW→

The animals were kind to their pets. They fed them well, and brought them to parks, where they could run and play with other pet people.

A group of gorillas opened a special school to teach people to "sit" and "lie down" and "heel" when they were told.

In the afternoon the animals washed and combed their pets, dressed them in ribbons and bows, and took them to a People Show. A panel of poodles looked at each person carefully, then gave a prize for the most beautiful pet in the kingdom.

Obedience School

"Step right up! Get your tickets
to the Circus!" cried the tiger. "See
wild men walk on all fours, wild women jump
through hoops of fire and wild children
juggle balls on their noses!"

"There's room for everyone.
High chairs for the rats,
low chairs for the cats,
and no chairs for the bats.

"Come one, come all! See the greatest
Wild People Show in the kingdom!"

FRESH
POPCORN
✕ ✕ ✕
SALTED or
ROASTED
PEANUTS

SOFT DRINKS
orangeade
lemonade
cherryade

ICE CREAM
chocolate
vanilla
strawberry
banana
mango
butterscotch
coffee

But the people weren't happy being pets
and beasts of burden.
They dreamed about the time when they held all the
keys and reins and leads.

At night some of them escaped and held a secret
meeting in the forest.

"Pigs and parrots stared at us all day,"
complained the zoo people.

"Monkeys rode on our backs," grumbled the
farmers.

"What about us?" cried the circus people.
"We had to dance whenever a tiger cracked his whip!"

"The animals have had their day!" the
zoo people yelled. "Now it's our turn again."

"Let's put the animals to work," shouted the farmers.

"And back in their doghouses!" agreed the pet people.

Everyone raised his hand.

"Down with the animals!" the people shouted as they ran back to the city.

So while the animals slept, the people crept on tiptoe
into the houses. Quiet as cats, they took all the keys,
then carried the sleeping animals back to the zoos and
circuses, the barns and stables.

The next morning when the animals woke up the world
was very different, for once again the kingdom belonged
to the people.

PUBLIC FOOTPATH
to the FOREST

Some other Picture Knight titles you may enjoy

The Picnic
Kady MacDonald Denton

Oodles of Noodles
Margaret Roc and Allan Stomann

Have You Seen My Cat?
Eric Carle

The Enormous Chocolate Pudding
Scoular Anderson